BEARCUB BIOS

MAE JEMISON

DOCTOR, SCIENTIST, AND ASTRONAUT

by Rachel Rose

Consultant: Beth Gambro
Reading Specialist, Yorkville, Illinois

BEARPORT PUBLISHING

Minneapolis, Minnesota

Teaching Tips

BEFORE READING

- Discuss what a biography is. What kinds of things might a biography tell a reader?
- Look through the glossary together. Read and discuss the words.
- Go on a picture walk, looking through the pictures to discuss vocabulary and make predictions about the text.

DURING READING

- Encourage readers to point to each word as it is read. Stop occasionally to ask readers to point to a specific word in the text.
- If a reader encounters an unknown word, ask them to look at the rest of the page. Are there any clues to help them understand?

AFTER READING

- Check for understanding.
  - Where was Mae Jemison born?
  - What does she do?
  - What does she care about?
- Ask the readers to think deeper.
  - If you met Mae, what question would you like to ask her? Why?

Credits:
Cover and title page, © lev radin/Shutterstock and © Oleg_Yakovlev/Shutterstock; 3, © Lachlan Cunningham/Getty Images; 5, © NASA; 7, © Stonel/Shutterstock; 8-9, © jejim/iStock; 11, © Bettmann/Getty Images; 12, © Interim Archives/Getty Images; 14-15, © NASA; 14 (inset), © BRUCE WEAVER/Getty Images; 16-17, © NC Collections/Alamy Stock Photo; 18, © Rawpixel.com/Shutterstock; 19, © Lachlan Cunningham/Getty Images; 21, © China Photos/Getty Images; 22, © Hum Images/Alamy Stock Photo; 23TL, © M.Aurelius/Shutterstock; 23TR, © AaronAmat/iStock; 23BL, © Ingus Kruklitis/Shutterstock; and 23BR, © Monkey Business Images/Shutterstock.

Library of Congress Cataloging-in-Publication Data

Names: Rose, Rachel, 1968– author. Title: Mae Jemison : doctor, scientist, and astronaut / by Rachel Rose. Description: Minneapolis, MN : Bearport Publishing Company, [2021] | Series: Bearcub bios | Includes bibliographical references and index. Identifiers: LCCN 2019060289 (print) | LCCN 2019060290 (ebook) | ISBN 9781642809817 (library binding) | ISBN 9781642809923 (paperback) | ISBN 9781647470036 (ebook) Subjects: LCSH: Jemison, Mae, 1956–Juvenile literature. | African American women astronauts—Biography—Juvenile literature. | Women astronauts—United States—Biography—Juvenile literature. Classification: LCC TL789.85.J46 R67 2021 (print) | LCC TL789.85.J46 (ebook) | DDC 629.450092 [B]—dc23 LC record available at https://lccn.loc.gov/2019060289 LC ebook record available at https://lccn.loc.gov/2019060290

For more information, write to Bearport Publishing, 5357 Penn Avenue South, Minneapolis, MN 55419.

Printed in the United States of America.

Contents

Flying into Space

Mae Jemison was very **excited**.

Her dream was coming true.

Mae was getting ready to fly into space!

NASA
GIBSON APT BROWN
LEE DAVIS JEMISON MOHRI

Mae's Life

Mae was born in Alabama.

Her family moved to Chicago when she was three.

Mae loved science.

She also loved to dance!

Mae danced with shoes like this.

Mae went to school here.

In college, Mae did all the things she liked.

She did science.

She became a doctor.

And she kept dancing!

Mae wanted to help people.

After she became a doctor, she went to Africa.

She helped sick people there.

Mae is a doctor!

ADULT FROG BOX
COMPARTMENT
FROG
ENVIRONMENTAL
UNIT
0-G STOWAGE
COMPARTMENT
CENTRIFUGE

Then, Mae went to **NASA**.

She wanted to be an **astronaut**.

NASA only takes the best people.

Mae was one of the best!

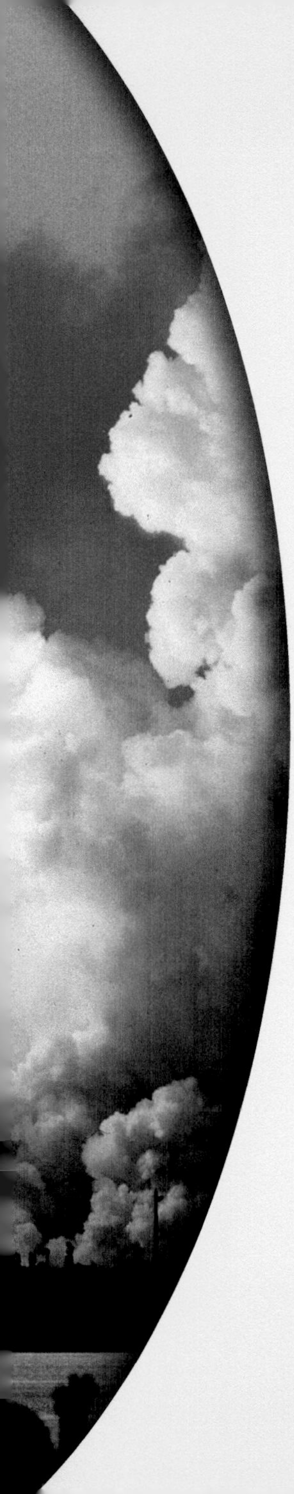

On September 12, 1992, Mae flew into space.

She was with six others.

Mae was the first African American woman in space!

The astronauts were in space for eight days.

Mae did **tests**.

She learned what happens to human bodies in space.

After Mae left NASA, she was a teacher.

She also started a science camp.

Mae wanted all kids to learn about science.

Mae still loves space travel.

She hopes people will be able to go even deeper into space.

She is working hard to make that dream come true.

Did You Know?

Born: October 17, 1956

Family: Dorothy (mother), Charlie (father), Ada (sister), Charles (brother)

When she was a kid: She went to the library a lot. She loved learning about the stars.

Special fact: She was once on a TV show.

Mae says: "The thing that I have done throughout my life is to do the best job that I can and to be me."

Life Connections

Mae works hard to make her dreams come true. What are your dreams? What can you do to make them come true?

Glossary

astronaut a person who travels into space

excited very happy about something

NASA the group in charge of the U.S. space program

tests things to answer questions or problems

Index

Read More

Castro, Rachel. *Mae Jemison (STEM Superstars).* Chicago: Norwood House (2020).

Strand, Jennifer. *Mae Jemison (Zoom In on Pioneering Explorers).* Minneapolis: Abdo Zoom (2017).

Learn More Online

1. Go to **www.factsurfer.com**
2. Enter "**Mae Jemison**" into the search box.
3. Click on the cover of this book to see a list of websites.

About the Author

Rachel Rose writes books for children. She teaches yoga, too. She lives in San Francisco with her husband and her dog, Sandy.